Little Women

Louisa May Alcott

Editor: Heather Hammonds
Cover Illustration: Terry Riley
Illustrations: Terry Riley
Typesetting: Midland Typesetters

Little Women
First published in 2008 by
Playmore Inc., Publishers,
58 Main Street, Hackensack, N.J. 07601

Printed in China

The Author
Louisa May Alcott
(1832–1888)

Louisa May Alcott was the second of four daughters of a Pennsylvanian poet, educational reformer, and philosopher. Her three sisters were to become the models for Meg, Beth, and Amy, three of the heroines of her best-known book *Little Women*. Much of Alcott's own character, of course, emerges in Jo—every young reader's champion.

Alcott first attracted attention with *Hospital Sketches* (1863), which told of her experiences as an army nurse in the American Civil War. But it was *Little Women* (1868) that brought her international fame. Her other works included the sequels *Good Wives*, *Little Men*, *Jo's Boys,* and *Aunt Jo's Scrap Bag*.

During her life, Alcott was involved in the women's rights movement and the fight against alcohol abuse.

Contents

Chapter 1
Christmas Won't Be Christmas

"Christmas won't be Christmas without presents," grumbled Jo March, who was sitting in front of the fire with her three sisters. Snow was falling outside.

"It's so dreadful to be poor," sighed Meg, the eldest, looking down at the old dress she was wearing.

"Some girls have everything," added Amy, the youngest of the family, moving her toes closer to the fire, "and we have nothing."

"We've got Father and Mother," interrupted Beth, who also saw the good things in life. "And we also have each other!"

"But we haven't got Father," interrupted Jo, "and we won't have him for a long time."

Father was away in the Civil War and that reminded the four March sisters of why Mother had suggested they shouldn't buy any presents this year.

"We shouldn't think about presents," she

had said, "while the men are fighting and dying in the war."

"But I'm sure Mother wouldn't mind if we spent a dollar on ourselves," said Meg, who worked as a governess to the wealthy King family. "To be sure, we have worked hard to earn it. I know I do—teaching those dreadful King children."

"You don't have half as hard a time as I do," complained Jo, "looking after old Aunt March. She's always moaning at me."

Amy wasn't going to be left out of the general complaints. "I don't believe any of you suffer as I do," she said. "I have to go to school each day with girls who laugh at my old dresses, joke how poor Father is, and say my nose looks funny."

"Really!" interrupted Meg, in her elder-sister fashion. "We must stop moaning at each other. And Jo, just remember that you are a young lady. Polite young ladies don't complain."

"I'm *not* a young lady!" snapped Jo. "I'd hate to think I'll grow up into a proper young lady who wears long gowns and is as proud as a peacock. It's bad enough being a girl when I really prefer boys' games and the work they do.

"Christmas won't be Christmas without presents."

I'll never get over the disappointment on discovering I was a girl and not a boy! I'm just dying to go and join Father on the battlefield."

Meg turned her attention to Amy. "And you shouldn't be so proud of the airs and graces you put on," she said. "You'll grow up into a very posh little goose, if you don't watch out."

Beth was feeling left out now. "If Jo is a tomboy and Amy is a goose, what am I?" she asked.

"You're an absolute dear," replied Meg. "You're the pet of the family. Everyone loves you."

There never were four more different girls than the March sisters.

"I'm not *a young lady!"*

Chapter 2
Little Women

Meg, the eldest of the March girls, was just sixteen. She was very pretty; plump and fair, with large eyes and lots of soft brown hair.

Tomboy Jo was fifteen. She was very tall, thin, and dark-skinned. She was rather like a young colt, with long legs that seemed to go in all directions at once.

Jo had sharp gray eyes which in turn could be fierce, funny, or thoughtful. She also had beautiful long, thick hair. Jo was rapidly growing up into a young woman and didn't like the idea at all. Quick tempered, sharp tongued, and restless, she had a pet rat called Scrabble.

Beth was a rosy, bright-eyed girl of thirteen. She was the quietest of all the girls. Painfully shy, the loves of her life were playing the piano and tending her three cats.

Amy was the youngest, and in her opinion, the most important of all the girls. She didn't see herself as a goose at all. She had beautiful blue eyes and blond curly hair that tumbled over her shoulders. Pale and slender, Amy carried herself like a true lady, even though she was only twelve. She was known to her family as *Her Ladyship*.

That afternoon, Mrs. March was out visiting and the girls were eagerly awaiting her return. Beth put Mother's slippers close to the fire. Mrs. March would be home in an hour, and Beth knew she would like warm slippers to put on.

"Those slippers are quite worn out," said Jo.

"I know what," said Beth. "We can spend our money on a nice new pair of slippers for Mother."

All the girls thought it was a lovely idea. They were on their feet and off to town in a jiff.

They were back with their present just as Mrs. March arrived home.

"Where have you been?" she asked.

"Just seeing friends in town," said Meg, who was the best actress in the family.

Mrs. March was the most motherly woman. How those four girls loved her, even when she was wearing her dull gray cloak and unfashionable bonnet. "Well, dearies," she said, giving each one a kiss. "How are we all?"

Now that Mother was home, there were no more moans. The four girls rushed around,

Putting Mother's slippers close to the fire

pulling up a chair for her right in front of the fire and putting the warmed-up slippers on her feet.

Mrs. March had a particularly happy smile on her face. "I've got a special treat for you after supper," she said.

The girls knew what that meant. A letter from Father must have arrived.

"Yes," she said, patting her pocket as if she had a big treasure inside it, "a nice long letter. I'll read it to you after supper."

Never was a supper cooked so fast. Never had the girls cleared up more quickly afterwards, either.

After supper, they all gathered around the fireplace again. Mother was in the big chair with Beth at her feet. Meg and Amy perched on each arm of the chair. Jo leaned on the back.

Mrs. March read out the letter. Father made no mention of the hardships of war, the dangers faced, or the terrible feelings of homesickness. Instead it was a hopeful letter, full of lively descriptions of camp life, marches, and military news.

The letter was written to Mrs. March. But at the end of it, Mr. March spoke of how much he loved and missed his daughters.

Mrs. March read out the letter.

Your love for me keeps me going in this sad war. It could be at least a year before I get home again. I cannot wait. It seems such a long time to be away from my darlings. I think of you all day long, and pray for you each night. Now, don't forget to work hard and do your duties. Help Mother in every way you can.

Meg, I know you will look after Mother. And Jo, you must learn to be a little more ladylike and keep your pet rat out of the kitchen. Beth you are already an angel, just like those lovely cats of yours. And Amy, perhaps you could try and be a little more humble and stop worrying about your nose. It's a beautiful nose.

I know you'll all try your hardest to be good. And I also know that I will always be so proud of my 'little women'.

Jo wasn't ashamed at the great tear that suddenly dropped off the end of her nose when she heard those last two words.

Amy hid her tears by burying here face in her mother's lap. "I am a selfish girl," she cried, thinking about how they had all been moaning that afternoon. "I will try to be better so I never disappoint Father again."

"We all will," said Meg.

"I shall try not to be so boyish," said Jo. "If he calls me one of his 'little women' then I shall do my best not to be so rough and wild."

Beth said nothing, but wiped away her tears and decided she would be quieter than ever.

Later that evening, there was music and singing. No one but Beth could get any music out of their ancient piano. Meg, who had a voice like a flute and Mrs. March, who sang like an angel, led the March family choir. Amy chirped along too, but Jo wandered through the song at her own pace and always came in at the wrong place.

The sound of their voices filled the room and brought cheer to the household at the end of the day.

Chapter 3
Christmas Day

Jo was the first to wake on Christmas morning, and she woke the other girls. They quickly dressed and rushed downstairs. Hannah, who had worked as a servant to the March family for many years, had already prepared the breakfast table. There was buckwheat cereal, fresh bread, and cream and muffins.

There was a parcel beside each of the girls' places, though Mother had said they were too poor this year to give presents. Mother herself was nowhere to be seen.

"Where is she?" Meg asked Hannah, who was really much more one of the family than a servant.

"Goodness knows," she replied. "Some poor creature came a-begging and your ma went off to see what was needed. There never was such a woman for looking after needy folk."

Soon after, Mrs. March returned. The children

Mother was nowhere to be seen.

ran to her and hugged her to bits. After they had all done with kissing her, thanking her, and wishing her a happy Christmas, Mother said she wanted a word with them.

"Not far away from here lies a poor woman with a newborn baby," she said. "There are six other children huddled in her bed to keep warm. They have no fire and nothing to eat. My children, will you give them your breakfast as a Christmas present?"

The girls were unusually hungry, having woken early. For a moment there was silence. Hannah could hear their tummies grumbling.

Then Jo spoke. "I'm glad you returned before we started eating."

"Yes," said Amy, picking up the cream and muffins.

"I'll take the buckwheat cereal," said Meg.

"I knew you'd do it," said Mrs. March. "We can have bread and milk when we get back. Then we'll see what we can find for Christmas dinner tonight."

The breakfast was packed up in a hamper and they all went off to deliver it to someone far needier than them. They stayed to watch the happiest Christmas breakfast they'd ever seen.

The happiest Christmas breakfast they'd ever seen

Back home, it was time for the girls to surprise Mrs. March. She had not expected any presents from her daughters and she was delighted with her new slippers. The girls were also thrilled with their presents. Mrs. March had made each one a new blouse to wear.

But there were more surprises, later that day. Their neighbor, Grandpa Laurence, had heard of their good deed at breakfast. He sent around his grandson, known to the girls as simply 'the Laurence boy', with a Christmas supper such as they had never seen.

The boy seemed very shy but he had also bought flowers for all the girls. He delivered the supper and flowers, and hurried off.

"His grandfather makes him work very hard," said Beth. "He keeps the boy shut up at home when he's not working or studying."

"What lovely flowers," said Meg. "Mother, can we ask him around for tea one day?"

"Of course," said Mrs. March. "He looks like a little gentleman to me."

Jo reluctantly agreed that it was kind of the boy to bring them flowers. But she wasn't going to admit she liked them. "I wish I could send them to Father," she said.

They all enjoyed their Christmas supper,

and the next morning there was more excitement. An invitation from old Mrs. Gardiner, another neighbor, had arrived. She had asked the two eldest girls, Meg and Jo, to attend her New Year's Eve dance.

"What shall we wear?" wondered Meg.

"What's the use of asking that?" replied Jo. "We'll have to go in our plain cotton dresses. We haven't got anything else."

"If only I had a silk dress," said Meg.

"Our cottons are quite good enough," said Jo, "except that mine has a tear and a small burn at the back."

"The front is all right," said Meg. "You'll just have to sit still with your back out of sight. But what about my gloves? They are so old and stained. And you can't go to a dance without nice gloves."

"If I've got to sit still all night," said Jo, "then you can just keep your gloves crunched up in your hands all the time, too."

Chapter 4
The Laurence Boy

New Year's Eve soon arrived. Meg and Jo, who was feeling very conscious of the burn mark on the back of her dress, were walked to the dance by Hannah.

When they arrived, they were met by Mrs. Gardiner. She greeted them and then handed them over to her six daughters. Meg knew them all quite well, so she was soon at ease talking to them. Jo, who despite her boyish ways was quite shy, went and stood by herself—her back to the wall, of course.

A few minutes later, Jo saw a tall ginger-haired fellow approaching her. She panicked, terrified that he was going to ask her to dance. How could she, with that burn mark?

She slipped behind the nearest curtain and found herself in a small recess. Unfortunately, another bashful person had chosen the same refuge. She found herself face-to-face with the Laurence boy.

Face-to-face with the Laurence boy

"Dear me!" stammered Jo, preparing to back out as quickly as she had bounced in. "I didn't know anyone else was here."

The boy laughed. "Stay if you like," he said.

"Shan't I disturb you?" she asked.

"Not a bit," he said. "I only came here because I didn't know many people."

"So did I," replied Jo.

"Did you enjoy the Christmas dinner I brought?" he asked.

"It was very kind of you, Master Laurence," she replied.

"It was Grandpa who sent it, Miss March," said the boy.

"Please, Master Laurence," said Jo, "I'm not Miss March. I'm only Jo."

"And I'm not Master Laurence—just Laurie," said the boy.

"What a strange name," said Jo, "Laurie Laurence."

"My real first name is Theodore, but I hate it," he explained.

"I hate my name too," said Jo. "I wish everyone would call me Jo instead of Josephine."

Just then the curtain swished aside and Laurie spotted Meg dancing. "Your sister is looking very pretty tonight," he remarked.

Jo looked out and saw that the ginger-haired boy was now dancing with Meg.

"He looks like a grasshopper having a fit," laughed Laurie.

Jo decided that she liked the Laurence boy. For a lad he was well-mannered, and she liked the fact that he was as tall as her. His dark hair was matched by equally dark eyes. "Why don't you go and dance?" she asked.

"I will if you come with me," said Laurie.

Poor Jo had to confess that she couldn't because of the burn mark on her dress.

"Never mind," said Laurie, "there's a corridor behind the curtains. We could dance there."

Jo felt at ease with Laurie now. In fact, they had several dances. They were still stepping out when Meg appeared to say that a carriage had arrived to take them home.

Of course, Beth and Amy were still awake when they got home. "Tell us everything," cried Beth. "Jo, did you fall in love with some brave soldier?"

"I might have done," said Jo. "I danced with so many handsome young men."

"She's fibbing," interrupted Meg. "She danced with the Laurence boy all night."

21

They had several dances.

"No I didn't!" fibbed Jo. "But I saw you with that horrible red-haired boy."

. So the gossip went on until everyone and everything at the ball had been discussed, and Meg, Jo, Beth, and Amy had finally fallen asleep.

Chapter 5
Bundles

After the New Year's Eve party, the holidays came to an end.

"I wish it was Christmas and New Year all the time," said Jo. "We could go to parties and drive home in smart carriages every night."

"Well, it's not possible," said Meg. "We must shoulder our bundles of problems and trudge along as cheerfully as Mother does."

Meg's "bundle" was the King family, where she was a governess to the troublesome children. Apart from the children, her main problem was the meager salary she got for the job. And the sight of all the fabulous ball gowns the young Kings wore made her very envious.

Jo's "bundle" was the ageing and irritable Aunt March, who had taken her on as her daily companion. Jo's ambition in life was to do something splendid; what it was, she had no idea at all. She was a restless spirit and found her work as companion to Aunt March rather trying.

A companion to Aunt March

In her heart, though, Jo liked the old lady. Besides, she had a wonderful library. The moment she nodded off after lunch, Jo would hurry off to bury herself in a book.

Jo stood her ground with Aunt March, too. One day she lost her temper at the old lady's tantrums and ran off home. Aunt March turned up on Jo's doorstep soon after, begging her to come back.

Since the war began Mrs. March had become very poor. Aunt March suggested she might adopt Jo to make life easier for her. Mrs. March had politely declined the offer, saying: "Rich or poor, me and my girls are all staying together."

It was always said that the decision cost the March family all hope of being remembered in the old lady's will.

Beth's "bundle" was shyness. She was so shy that it was decided that Mr. March could teach her at home. When he went away to the war, Beth faithfully went on with her studies by herself.

Beth was still a child, and she had six dolls to look after. She cherished them all, even the ugly and damaged ones. She set up a hospital for the sick dolls.

As for Amy, if anyone had asked her what her "bundle" or main trouble in life was, she would have said: "My nose." When she was a baby she had fallen over and hurt it. Since then, it had become rather flat. All the pinching in the world could not give it an aristocratic point. No one minded the nose except Amy. And it was doing its best to grow.

Amy's great talent was art. Her teachers complained that instead of doing sums, she spent her day drawing and painting. But she got away with it. She had the happy skill of being able to please people without too much effort.

No one minded the nose except Amy.

As the youngest, Amy was rather spoilt. Yet, any vanity she had was kept under control by the fact that she had to wear her cousin's hand-me-down clothes, which were unbecoming and unfashionable.

Both the older girls adopted a younger sister to especially care for. Meg kept a close eye on young Amy, and Jo was Beth's mentor. Jo was the only one privy to shy Beth's most secret thoughts.

Jo was the storyteller of the four. Each evening when they were at home together, one of the girls would ask Jo to tell them what she had done that day. Jo always had a story to tell.

"Today Aunt March gave me a lecture on my sins," she began one evening. "I was reading aloud to her from a most boring book. It must have been boring because she kept nodding off. Each time I saw her head begin to drop, I cheered up. I knew I would soon be able to read one of my own books."

Jo's sisters enjoyed her stories very much.

For the most part, they were happy children. And when they felt down on their luck because they were poor, Mrs. March also had a story for them.

Mrs. March spent several hours a day working at the Soldiers' Aid Society where she made clothes for the poor people whose fathers were fighting in the war. One day when the four girls were arguing and complaining about their lot, she told them a special tale.

"I met an old man today," she began, "and I told him I was worried about Father. I was just wondering what we would do if he didn't come back from the war. I asked the man if he had any children in the army.

"He said: 'Yes, ma'am. I had four, but two were killed, one is a prisoner, and the other is very sick. I'm going to see him in hospital.'"

Mrs. March said she told the man that he had given a great deal for his country and he replied: "Nothing more than I ought. I gave my boys and I gave them free."

All the girls fell silent after that inspiring story.

"And I can tell you another story," said Mrs. March. "It's about four girls. They always had enough to eat and drink, and good enough clothes to wear. They were loved by their parents and many friends, yet, they were constantly saying: 'If only we had this . . . if only we had that.' They had quite forgotten how much they

An inspiring story

already had. One day they were visited by a kindly witch. The four girls asked the witch how they could be really happy. The witch told them just to count their blessings and be grateful."

The four girls now knew exactly who their mother was talking about. But before they could say a word, Mrs. March continued her story.

"So the girls took the witch's advice. And do you know what? They quickly realized how well-off they were. One discovered that rich people could be as unhappy as the poor. The second, although poor, realized that she was a great deal happier than a certain old aunt. The third came to see that helping her mother to get the dinner was better than having to go out into the streets and beg for food. The fourth found out that vanity was a very expensive habit."

The four girls were now laughing at how their mother described all their weaknesses in one story.

"And how does the story end?" asked Jo.

"Oh," said Mrs. March, "they all agreed to stop complaining about their bundles in life. And after that, they all became very cheerful girls who never complained about anything again. Of course, they lived happily ever after."

Chapter 6
A Lonely Boy

"Jo! What in the world are you going to do now?" asked Meg one snowy afternoon, as her sister came clumping through the hall.

"Not being a pussycat, I can't doze by the fireside," replied Jo, who was carrying a brush and shovel. "I like adventure and I'm going to find some."

Meg shook her head and left Jo to her own devices.

Once outside, Jo began digging a path through the snow towards the Laurence's house next door. A low hedge separated the March and Laurence houses. The March house was a shabby brown building. The Laurence house was a stately stone mansion.

Jo thought how sad it was that such a grand house should be so quiet. In the March garden, Beth and Amy were now throwing snowballs at each other. Yet no children were frolicking on the snow-covered lawn next door. No

A Lonely Boy

A stately stone mansion

motherly face ever stood smiling at the windows. And few people ever went in or out of the house.

To Jo, the Laurence house seemed a kind of enchanted palace. Since meeting Laurie at the New Year's Eve party, she was determined to visit him at home.

Jo waited until she heard Grandpa Laurence leave the house and then dug the path right up to the hedge. Looking up, she saw the sad face of Laurie at a window. He seemed to be watching Beth and Amy.

"Poor boy, all alone," thought Jo, as she rolled up a small snowball and threw it at the window where Laurie was.

Laurie was startled. But when he saw who had thrown the snowball, a huge smile crossed his face. "Hello Jo," he called down.

"How are you?" replied Jo.

"I've had a cold," he said, "so I haven't been out for a few days. I'm so bored."

"Haven't you a friend who can read a book to you?" asked Jo.

"I don't know anyone," he replied.

"You know me," said Jo.

"So I do," replied Laurie. "Will you come over?"

"I'll need to ask Mother first," she said, and hurried back to her house.

A few minutes later Jo, carrying a dish of blancmange under one arm and Beth's three kittens under the other, arrived on Laurie's doorstep. She was shown into his room by a maid.

"Mother sends her love," she said. "Beth thought you might like to see her kittens, and Meg sent the blancmange."

Laurie was quite overcome by the kindness of the March family. "Meg is the pretty one, isn't she?" he asked. "And Beth is the rosy one. The curly one is Amy."

"I didn't know you knew all my sisters," said Jo.

"Oh, I don't," said Laurie, blushing. "But when I'm alone up here, I can't help looking over at your house. You always seem to be having such fun together."

"You must come and join us sometimes," said Jo. "Beth will sing for you. Amy will dance. And Meg and I will tell you funny stories. Would your grandpa let you come?"

"He would if your mother asked him," said the boy. "He might not look a very kind man. He is though. He lets me do what I like, but he worries that I might be a bother to strangers."

"We aren't strangers!" cried Jo. "We are neighbors and you won't be a bother at all."

Laurie asked Jo if she liked school.

"I don't go to school," said Jo. "I'm a companion for my aunt; a dear, cross old soul she is too."

Jo loved talking to people about her aunt. "She's a fidgety old lady, has a fat poodle, a parrot that talks Spanish, and a library to die for."

Then Jo told Laurie about a prim old gentle-man who once fell in love with Aunt March. One day he came in and Aunt March's parrot pecked the man's wig from his head. Laurie couldn't stop laughing after that. The tears were running down his cheeks.

Jo soon discovered that she and Laurie shared a love of books.

"I'll show you Grandpa's library," said Laurie. "He's not here so there's nothing to be frightened about."

"I'm not afraid of him," said Jo.

"I don't believe you are," replied Laurie. "Come on."

The library was a huge room filled with not just books, but also statues and paintings, and cabinets containing coins and curiosities.

Laurie couldn't stop laughing.

"What a place," Jo sighed. "You ought to be the happiest boy in the world to live here."

Before Laurie could answer, the doorbell went.

"Mercy me! It's your grandfather!" cried Jo.

Chapter 7
Grandpa Laurence

"I thought you said you weren't afraid of my grandfather," Laurie said to Jo, when he saw how nervous she looked at the thought of meeting the old man.

"I'm not!" Jo snapped in return.

Unfortunately for Jo, Grandpa Laurence had a habit of moving fast and silently around his house. He had good hearing too.

"So you're not afraid of me, eh?" said a gruff voice behind them.

Jo turned around to find Grandpa Laurence looming above her. She could hardly see his eyes for the thick bushy brows.

"No, sir," she said quietly.

The gentleman gave a short laugh and shook hands with her. "I knew your grandfather, Jo," he said. "You've got his spirit. He was a fine man, a brave and honest one too. I was proud to be his friend."

"So you're not afraid of me, eh?"

"Thank you, sir," said Jo, recovering her courage.

"And what have you been doing to my grandson?" he asked. "He can't stop smiling."

"Nothing, sir, just being neighborly," replied Jo.

"You think he needs cheering up, eh?"

"He does seem a little lonely," said Jo. "Seeing young folks would do him good. We are only girls, but we'd be glad to be good neighbors with all of you."

Grandpa Laurence was silent for a moment. He knew that Jo was speaking the truth. Laurie was lonely. The boy did need cheering up. He called for tea to be served in the music room. Jo immediately spotted the piano. "Can you play, Laurie?" she asked.

"A little," answered Laurie.

"Then you must play for us," said Jo.

Laurie sat down at the piano and began playing. He played beautifully and how Jo wished that Beth could have heard him. Suddenly, Grandpa Laurence got up and quietly told Laurie it was time to stop playing. It seemed that the music had upset the old man.

After tea, Grandpa Laurence made Jo promise she would visit again. And he promised to call on Mrs. March.

Just as she was leaving, Jo asked Laurie a question. "Why did your grandfather stop you playing the piano?"

"I'll tell you some day," said Laurie, "but not now."

When Jo got home, the first thing she asked her mother was why Grandpa Laurence didn't like Laurie playing the piano.

Mrs. March wasn't sure. But she thought it was something to do with Laurie's mother. "Perhaps Laurie's natural talent as a musician just reminds Grandpa Laurence of sad days. You must remember that Laurie's parents both died when he was a little child."

Playing the piano

"Then we must all be nice to him," said Jo. "If he comes over you can be his Mother too."

"Your friend is very welcome," said Mrs. March.

Grandpa Laurence didn't just call on Mrs. March. He became a regular visitor, much to the joy of all the girls except Beth, who was much too shy to talk to him.

The only other problem for the March Family was that they were poor and the Laurence family was rich. The girls didn't like accepting favors and presents that they could not return.

After a while, even that didn't matter. Grandpa Laurence clearly saw himself as their true benefactor. He often said how grateful he was for Mrs. March's motherly care and the cheerful company of the girls.

Laurie, of course, adored them all. Never having had a mother or sisters, he just loved them so much.

Chapter 8
Beth's Special Present

The friendship between the March and Laurence families grew even stronger. Meg was forever popping over to the Laurence house. Jo spent most of her life buried in the library. And Amy loved to copy the wonderful pictures there. Only shy Beth missed out. Secretly, she yearned to go over and play on Grandpa Laurence's grand piano. But she daren't ask, and no one could persuade her to go and ask him.

Eventually Grandpa Laurence got to hear about Beth's love of music. The cunning old man thought up a plan to tempt her to come and play on his piano.

First, he started bringing up the topic of music whenever Beth was about. He talked about the great singers he had met and the fine pianos he had seen. Beth found it impossible not to listen to him. Each time he came to the house and started talking about music, she began to lose some of her shyness.

Talking about music

At first she would sit in a far corner of the room. But the more interesting the things Grandpa Laurence talked about, the closer she came. Within a few days she was quite happy to lean on the back of Grandpa Laurence's chair. He pretended not to notice her. Then he played his final card on a visit to the March household.

"Mrs. March," he said one day, "do you know anyone who loves playing the piano? Our grand piano suffers for want of use. Would any of your girls like to pop over sometimes and play . . . just to keep it in tune? They could run over at any time. There would be no need to ask permission. They wouldn't even have to see me or any of the servants. Just walk in the door."

Mrs. March, Meg, Jo, and Amy all looked at Beth. The temptation was just too much, even for Beth.

"I like to play the piano," she said. "But are you sure I won't disturb someone?"

"Not a soul," replied Grandpa Laurence. "As far as you are concerned, the house would be empty. Besides, you will be doing me a favor."

Grandpa Laurence reached out and squeezed Beth's hand. "I once had a little girl with big blue eyes like you," he said.

Beth didn't see the tears that formed in the old man's eyes as he quickly said his goodbyes and left.

The next day Beth walked over to the Laurence house. She quickly found the piano in the drawing room and began playing. In a moment, she had forgotten all her shyness. The beautiful grand piano had become her friend.

After that first day, Beth went to the house whenever she could. She really thought that the house was empty. She never knew that Grandpa Laurence often quietly opened the door of his study to listen to her fine playing. She never saw Laurie on guard outside the drawing room to keep the servants from disturbing her.

Beth was so grateful to Grandpa Laurence that she made him a pair of fine slippers. The day after she gave them to him, a letter arrived for her. It was addressed to Miss Elizabeth March and it came with a very special present —a small piano.

"For me?" she gasped.

"Yes, all for you, my precious," replied Jo. "Isn't it splendid of Grandpa Laurence?"

Then Beth read the letter.

"For me?"

Dear Madam,
I have had many pairs of slippers in my life,
but I never had any as nice as yours. The piano is
for you. It belonged to the granddaughter I lost.
Your grateful friend and humble servant,
James Laurence

Beth was delighted. She had never been called Madam before. And she had definitely never had a humble servant before. It all sounded so grown-up.

She quickly tried the piano. It had been newly tuned and was in apple-pie order. The other girls had never seen such a happy expression on her face as she started to play with that loving touch of hers.

Afterwards, Beth ran to thank Grandpa Laurence. She knocked on his study door.

"Come in," said a gruff voice.

For a moment, Beth was frightened again. But she knew what she wanted to do and shyness was not going to stop her. She pushed open the door and ran to Grandpa Laurence, throwing both arms around his neck and kissing him.

If the roof of the house had suddenly blown off, Grandpa Laurence couldn't have been more astonished.

Chapter 9
Skating on Thin Ice

With four girls living under one roof, there were times when they had their arguments.

One night Jo and the two other older girls arranged to go to the theater with Laurie. They decided the play they were to see was too grown up for Amy.

Amy was furious at being left out. "I shall come with you anyway," she said, stamping her feet in anger.

"You can't," said Jo. "Laurie has booked the tickets for tonight. There won't be a spare seat now."

Amy sat on the floor at the foot of the stairs and began to cry. Just then, Laurie arrived. Meg and Beth hurried down the stairs to meet him. Jo followed them.

"You'll be sorry for this, Jo March," sobbed Amy. "Just you see if you aren't!"

When the three girls got home that evening, they found Amy reading in the parlor. She

Amy began to cry.

kept her eyes on her book and ignored them completely.

Now, Jo had been writing a story during the last few weeks. She kept the manuscript in the parlor desk. She was so proud of it. The family was sure she would get it published one day.

Whenever she came into the house, Jo would check to see that the manuscript was safe and sound. But that night she looked in the desk and saw it was missing.

She immediately turned to Amy. "What have you done with it?" she demanded to know.

"Nothing," Amy replied.

"Where is it, then?" said Jo.

"I don't know," snapped Amy.

"That's a fib!" shouted Jo, taking Amy by the shoulders and threatening to shake her.

"I haven't got it," insisted Amy.

"You know something about it then," said Jo, "and you'd better tell me quickly, or else."

"Scold me as long as you like," Amy cried angrily. "You'll never get your silly story . . . because I burnt it!"

"You burnt it!" shrieked Jo.

"Yes," said Amy. "I said you'd be sorry for not taking me to the theater."

"You wicked, wicked girl!" cried Jo. "That was my only copy. I can never write it again. There were months of work in that book. I'll never forgive you as long as I live!"

Jo stormed out of the room, just as Mrs. March arrived home. When she heard what had happened, she quickly told Amy what a terrible thing she had done. "That book," she said, "was Jo's pride and joy."

Amy knew then that no one would love her again until she had asked to be pardoned for her crime. At breakfast the next day, she walked up to Jo and asked for forgiveness. "It was a terrible thing I did," she said in a low voice.

"I shall never forgive you!" replied Jo.

After that, Jo completely ignored Amy. The silence between the two girls was as cold as the ice that had frozen over the river.

Then one morning, Laurie invited Jo and Amy to go ice-skating. He hoped they might make their peace. The three of them trooped down to the river. Jo turned her back on Amy while Laurie went ahead to check the ice was safe.

A moment later, Laurie shouted back. "Keep near the river bank. The ice is thicker.

It's too dangerous to skate in the middle."

Jo heard the warning perfectly clearly. But Amy, who was still busy tying up her ice-skates, didn't hear a word.

Jo zigzagged off away down the river close to the bank. "Amy can take care of herself!" she said bitterly.

Laurie was already skating around the bend and Jo was a short distance behind him. Amy finished putting on her skates and set off, trying to catch up with the others. She immediately struck out for the smoother ice in the middle of the river.

Jo suddenly had a strange feeling of danger. Something told her to turn around. Just as she did, she saw Amy throw up her arms and crash through the ice. Jo's heart froze with terror. She tried to call Laurie but her voice had gone. Her feet seemed stuck to the ice. She couldn't move.

Suddenly, she saw Laurie race past her. He had also seen Amy go through the ice and was speeding to her rescue.

"Jo! Get a long stick!" he yelled.

At last, Jo leapt into action, doing everything Laurie ordered.

Laurie supported Amy with his arms while

Crashing through the ice

Jo crashed into the bushes and grabbed a broken tree branch. She emerged, cut and bruised, a few moments later. Inch by inch, they hauled Amy out of the water and onto the stronger ice.

Poor Amy was more frightened than hurt. Shivering, dripping, and crying, she was taken home. She had a hot bath and went straight to bed.

"Is she alright?" Jo asked Mother that evening.

"Quite safe," replied Mrs. March. "She probably won't even get a cold. You did the right thing in getting her home so quickly."

Jo burst into tears and threw here arms around her mother. "If Amy dies," she cried, "it will be my fault. It's my dreadful temper. I should have forgiven her when she asked. Instead I left her behind to look after herself on the ice."

Mrs. March hugged her daughter warmly. "You know what you must do now," she said. "Amy is going to be fine. But she might like to see you. She is truly sorry about what she did to your story."

Jo left her mother and went upstairs. Amy was still sleeping.

"If you had died, I'd never have forgiven

myself," she whispered quietly. "How could I be so wicked?"

Jo began to stroke Amy's long blond hair. The little girl opened her eyes and held out her arms with a smile that went straight to Jo's heart. Neither said a word as they hugged each other closely.

Everything was forgiven and forgotten.

Chapter 10
Lazy Days

Summer was a holiday for all the girls. Aunt March had set off for her summer tour, so Jo was free of the old lady for a while. Meg also had a few weeks off from teaching the King children. Amy was only too delighted to be on her school holidays.

"I'm going to lie in bed and do nothing all summer," announced Meg.

"Hum!" said Jo. "I shall be sitting under the apple tree reading all summer, and going on the river with Laurie."

Beth said she would be lying about a great deal too. Amy said she was going to do nothing but work on her art.

But it didn't quite work out as they had planned.

Meg lay in bed until ten o'clock in the morning and got downstairs in time for a solitary breakfast. That breakfast did not taste half

Summer was a holiday.

as nice as the usual ones where everyone ate, laughed, and chatted together.

The room seemed lonely. Jo usually put out vases of flowers each day. Now there were no flowers, and Beth had not done her usual dusting either.

Jo spent her first day on the river bank reading a book. But she soon caught the sun and had a badly burnt nose.

Beth did mean to tidy her closet and sort through her clothes. But after emptying everything onto the floor, she decided to have a sleep. By the time she awoke it was time for bed. All her clothes remained in a pile on the floor.

Amy did manage to do one drawing of an oak tree.

And so it went on for the next few days. Soon, the girls began to get bored with doing nothing. Each day seemed to be getting longer and longer. At the end of the first week, each one admitted that they were glad it was over.

Now, Mrs. March had a great sense of humor. She knew the girls would soon tire of doing very little. So she played a little trick.

On the Saturday morning, the girls came down for breakfast and found a very unfamiliar state of affairs. The kitchen stove fire was out. There was no breakfast ready at all. There was no sign of Hannah, and Mother was nowhere to be seen.

"Mercy on us!" cried Jo. "What has happened?"

Meg ran upstairs to Mother's room. There she was, still in bed. "Hannah's sick," said Mother, "so she's got the day off. As for me, I've decided to follow your example. I'm not going to do anything for a while. As from today, I'm on holiday too."

When Meg came downstairs again and told the others, there was disappointment for a moment. Then they all looked at each other and started laughing.

"Thank goodness!" said Jo. "I hate doing nothing but reading. Now we can look after Mother and let her have a holiday."

Meg agreed. "It's so boring doing nothing," she said.

Beth and Amy heartily agreed.

"I'm going to light the stove," said Amy.

"And I'll cook Mother's breakfast," said Beth.

Meg said she would carry it upstairs on a tray, so Mother could eat it in bed for a change.

Jo said she would start cleaning up the house and putting fresh flowers in the vases

"I'm on holiday too."

again. "Lounging around doing nothing is just not fun," she said.

They worked hard for the rest of that summer. They even divided up the garden into four quarters, so each girl had their own plot to look after. Meg grew roses. Jo experimented with sunflowers. Beth planted sweet peas and pansies. Amy built a bower and planted it with honeysuckle.

So that summer, the girls were busier than ever. And they were happier than ever too.

Chapter 11
Secrets

"Finished!" cried Jo excitedly.

Jo had secretly been continuing with her writing during the summer and now her first story was ready. She rolled up the pages, tied them with a red ribbon and caught an omnibus into town. It was like a secret mission. She was determined that no one would see her go.

She reached her destination, pulled her hat down over her eyes, and entered a building with several nameplates on a board outside. One was for a dentist, and another was for a local newspaper. Ten minutes later she emerged, only to bump straight into Laurie.

"Oh, where have you been?" he asked.

"To the dentist," she answered, as a blush reddened her cheeks.

"Are you sure?" asked Laurie, in a knowing sort of way.

"Of course," said Jo. "I may have a tooth out next week."

It was like a secret mission.

"Your teeth are perfect," said Laurie. "Jo, you're up to some mischief. Where have you really been?"

Jo was bursting to tell Laurie the truth in any case. "I have just shown one of my stories to the editor of the newspaper," she said, hardly able to contain her excitement. "He'll tell me next week if he can publish it. I don't suppose anything will come of it."

"Of course it will," said Laurie. "I'm sure your stories are better than William Shakespeare's. We'll all feel so proud of our little authoress."

"Don't you dare tell anyone," said Jo. "It's our secret for now."

Laurie promised and they set off home together.

A few days later, Meg was looking out of the drawing room window when she saw a very excited Jo arrive home, with Laurie chasing her. He eventually caught up with her in Amy's flower bower. What went on there Meg couldn't see, but shrieks of laughter were heard, followed by the murmur of voices and a great flapping of a newspaper.

"What shall we do with Jo?" said Meg. "She does not behave like a young lady."

"What shall we do with Jo?"

"I hope she never will," said Beth. "She's so funny and lovely just as she is."

Jo and Laurie eventually came into the room. Jo settled into a large armchair and started to read the newspaper.

"What's in the newspaper?" asked Meg. "Anything interesting?"

"Just a story," replied Jo, "but not much of one."

"Read it to us," said Meg. "That will keep you out of mischief. What's it about?"

"A romance," replied Jo.

Jo settled back and read the story. The girls listened with interest. The tale was romantic and a bit sad. Most of the characters died by the end of the story, but everyone enjoyed it. When it was over, Beth asked who wrote it.

Jo sat up straight, cast aside the newspaper and announced in an excited and proud voice: "Me!"

"I knew it! I knew it!" cried Beth. "Oh Jo, I am so proud of you."

All three girls were absolutely delighted. Meg just couldn't believe it until she saw the words beneath the story:

By Miss Josephine March

"Well I never," said Hannah, when she was told about it.

Eventually, Mrs. March heard the commotion and came in. How proud she was. "Will you be doing some more?" she asked.

"The newspaper man wants me to write another one," said Jo. "He won't pay me for the first one. That was just practice, he said. But if he publishes another one, then he'll pay me. Who knows, I might earn a good living and be able to help you all."

Meg just couldn't believe it.

"I hope you do," said Meg.

"Oh, how I wish," said Jo, "that I could fix things for you all, just like I do for the heroes and heroines of my stories. If I had my way, some rich relation would leave us a fortune. You'd all marry a prince and Father would become the president."

"Never mind," said Mrs. March. "Our fortunes will get better some day. And Jo, we must send a copy of the story to Father. To think, he has an author for a daughter!"

Chapter 12
A Telegram

The next day Hannah came into the drawing room with a telegram from Washington.

Mrs. March snatched the envelope and ripped it open. She read the two lines it contained and slumped back into her chair, as white as a sheet.

Jo rushed across and took the telegram and read it out.

Dear Mrs. March,
    Your husband is very ill. Come at once.

It was signed by the officer in charge of Washington's main hospital.

"I must go at once, but it may be too late," said Mrs. March, with a sob.

All the girls began to cry.

"Now, now," said Hannah, taking charge. "We can't waste time crying. We must get your things ready straight away."

All the girls began to cry.

"You're right, Hannah," said Mrs. March. "Be calm girls. Let me think. Right! Now Laurie, send a telegram saying I am coming. The next train goes tomorrow morning. I'll catch that one."

Laurie rushed out and took his pony into town to send the telegram.

Meanwhile, Mrs. March was thinking about money. How could she afford to travel to Washington? A message was sent to Aunt March. A good sum of money came by return delivery. But there was a note from the old lady too.

I reluctantly enclose some money for your travel. But I must remind you that I warned you it was absurd for Mr. March to go to war. I always said no good would come of it.

As far as Aunt March was concerned, no good would come of anything!

Soon after, the doorbell rang. Meg answered it. The caller was John Brooke, who was Laurie's tutor. He offered to escort Mrs. March to Washington.

"How kind of you," said Meg. "Mother will accept, I'm sure."

Indeed she did. Mrs. March also accepted Grandpa Laurence's offer to be the children's guardian while she was away.

The rest of the day was spent making plans for the trip. It was only noticed later that Jo had gone missing. She returned late in the afternoon and handed her mother twenty-five dollars.

"My dear," said an astonished Mrs. March. "Where did that come from? You hadn't a cent this morning. I hope you haven't done anything rash."

"No," said Jo. "It's mine. I didn't beg, borrow, or steal it either. I only sold something that was mine to sell."

As she spoke, Jo took off her bonnet to reveal that her hair had been shorn truly short.

"You hair!" cried Mrs. March. "Your beautiful hair has gone!"

"I sold it to a wigmaker," Jo said quietly. "It's my contribution to making Father comfortable and bringing him home."

"Oh, my lovely daughter," said Mrs. March. "You shouldn't have done it."

"What's a few strands of hair," replied Jo. "It won't affect the fate of the nation. Besides, it will be good for my vanity. I was getting far too

"Your beautiful hair has gone!"

boastful about how long and glossy my hair had become."

How the other girls laughed at that.

But late that night, Jo couldn't get to sleep. Suddenly she let out a great sob. Beth and Amy were asleep, but Meg heard her. "What are you crying for?" she asked. "Are you crying for Father?"

"No," said Jo, bursting into tears.

"What then?" asked Meg.

"My hair," howled Jo. "I'm not sorry I cut it off to raise money for Father. I'd do it again tomorrow. It's only my vanity. My vanity is crying for my lost hair. It's tears for my lost beauty."

***

In the cold light of the next morning, the girls said their goodbyes to Mother.

"Goodbye, my darlings," said Mrs. March, with tears in her eyes. "God bless and keep you all well."

She kissed each one and then boarded the Laurence's carriage that was to take her to the station. As the horses pulled away, Mrs. March looked back at her family. They were all waving.

As the carriage turned the corner, the last thing she saw was the girls' four bright faces, and behind them like bodyguards, Grandpa Laurence, faithful Hannah, and the devoted Laurie.

Chapter 13
A Life and Death Battle

It was several days before the girls heard news of Father. He was responding to treatment and doing quite well. But now there was another cause for concern at home . . .

Mrs. March often visited poor families in the neighborhood, and one of her favorite families was the Hummels. With Mother away, it was Meg's duty to go and see that the Hummels were alright.

"I can't go today," complained Meg. "I'm too tired. Can you go Jo?"

"No," said Jo. "I've still got a cold. I don't want to make the Hummels's baby worse; I think she is sickening for something already. Let's leave it until tomorrow."

Meg agreed. But unknown to any of them, sweet Beth decided she would go and see the Hummels. She knew how much they liked visits. No one saw her leave the house with a basket full of food, and odds and ends for the

poor children. It was a very cold autumn afternoon and she already had a chill coming on.

Beth was only gone a little while. When
she returned home, she hadn't been missed by
the three girls. Instead of going to see them,
she went to Mrs. March's medicine chest. It
was there that Jo discovered her.

"Beth, you look awful," she said. "What's
wrong?"

"Jo, you've had scarlet fever, haven't you?"
said Beth.

"Yes," replied Jo. "So hopefully I'll never
get it again."

"Well, something dreadful happened just a
little while ago," said Beth, very quietly.

Jo listened as Beth explained how she had
gone to the Hummel house and found their
baby very ill.

"How is she now?" asked Jo.

"She's dead," cried Beth, bursting into tears.
"She died in my arms. She gave a little cry and
trembled, and then lay very still. I just held
her until the doctor came. She died of scarlet
fever! The doctor sent me home immediately.
He said I might catch it."

"No you won't," insisted Jo, hugging her
sister close. "Even if you do, it will be like me.

"Something dreadful happened."

You'll just be sick for a while. If only Mother was here . . ."

A few days later, Beth complained of a headache and a sore throat. She lay on her bed feeling very sick, her forehead hot. Jo went to get Hannah. She knew all about illnesses.

Hannah came upstairs and took one look, before sending for Dr. Bangs. "It looks like scarlet fever to me," she said. "Amy hasn't had scarlet fever yet, has she? So it's best we send her to Aunt March for a while. Don't let her in here. And keep Laurie and Grandpa Laurence away."

Amy was furious when she was told she would have to go and stay with the old lady. She shouted and pleaded. She did go in the end, but only after Laurie promised he'd come and see her every day. Laurie was terribly upset about Beth because she was his special pet.

Now Jo was worrying about whether Mother should be told. Hannah said it was best to wait rather than upset Mrs. March even more. The doctor arrived soon after. He thought Beth could have caught the fever from the baby. But, with luck, it might turn out to be just a slight attack.

He was wrong. In the next few days, Beth's condition worsened. Jo devoted herself to Beth

The doctor arrived soon after.

day and night. Meg was frightened, and begged to be allowed to write to Mother. Hannah just told her to wait a while.

How dark the days seemed now. Laurie haunted the March house like a restless ghost, wishing he could go and see Beth. Grandpa Laurence locked his grand piano because he could not bear to remember how Beth charmed him with her music. Meg often sat in the drawing room with tears in her eyes, praying for Beth.

Upstairs, Jo sat beside Beth's sickbed. For the first time, she truly understood the beauty and sweetness of Beth's character. Beth was a girl who was so generous that she lived her life for others. Now she was in danger of losing that life.

Everyone missed Beth. The milkman, the baker, the grocer, and the butcher all asked daily about her health. Everyone was astonished at how many friends shy little Beth had made without them knowing about it.

The news about Beth's health was bad. Within a few days she had lost consciousness. She was tossing and turning, muttering words that had no meaning. Dr. Bangs came twice a day. Hannah and Jo sat up with her all night.

The first day of December was wintry and
cold. A bitter wind was blowing and the snow
was falling heavily. Dr. Bangs called early and
held Beth's hot little hand in his for a moment.
Then he whispered to Hannah, "If Mrs. March
can leave her husband, then she'd better be
sent for. Even now, she might be too late."

Chapter 14
Hold on to Me, Jo!

Jo raced to town to send the telegram. On the way back she met Laurie.

"What's the matter?" he asked.

"I've sent a telegram to bring Mother home," said Jo, beginning to cry. "Beth is very poorly. She doesn't know us any more. She can't even talk. Nobody loves Beth like I do. I can't let her go. She can't die!"

As the tears poured down her face, Jo stretched out her hand in a helpless sort of way. Laurie took it in his. "I'm here," he whispered. "Hold on to me, Jo!"

And she did hold on. The warm grasp of Laurie's hand comforted her sore heart. He stroked her head as he remembered Mrs. March had used to do. Then he gave her some surprise news.

"I've already sent for your mother," he said.

"I don't understand," sobbed Jo.

"I know Hannah told us to wait," he continued,

Laurie took her hand in his.

"but I just thought she was wrong. I sent a telegram yesterday. The good news is that I've had an answer. She'll be here first thing tomorrow morning."

Jo let out a joyful cry. "Oh Laurie! How wonderful! Laurie, you're an angel. How shall I ever thank you?"

Jo ran back to the house to tell everyone the good news. "Mother's coming. Mother's coming!" she cried.

Everyone rejoiced except Beth. She lay in a heavy stupor, unconscious of hope, joy, doubt, or danger. She was a sad sight. Her rosy face was now a ghostly white. Her hands were weak and wasted. Her hair lay in tangles across her pillow. The only word she had uttered all day was: "Water!"

Night fell and still it snowed, and the bitter wind blew. Jo and Meg were now sitting on either side of Beth's sickbed. The last thing the doctor had said was that Beth could slip either way now.

"If she lives," whispered Meg, "I shall never complain about anything ever again."

"I wish I had no heart," said Jo. "It aches so."

The clock struck twelve. Both girls were watching Beth. They thought they had seen a change pass over her white face. The house was as still as death. Only the sound of the wailing wind outside broke the deep hush.

Another hour went by. Nothing happened except Laurie's departure to meet the dawn train from Washington.

Another hour passed. It was past two when Jo, who had been looking out of the window at the blinding snow, heard a movement by the bed.

Quickly turning, she saw Meg kneeling over

Beth could slip either way now.

Beth. A dreadful, cold fear passed over Jo. Had Beth died? Was Meg too afraid to tell her? She looked again at Beth's face. The flush of the fever seemed to have gone and her face was now in utter peace.

Jo let out a cry, and then kissed her sister on the forehead. "Goodbye, my dear Beth. Goodbye," she whispered, so sure that her dearest sister had left this life.

Just then, Hannah awoke and went across to the bedside. First she held Beth's hands and then she listened at her chest, to see if she was breathing. "Praise be!" she cried. "The child is breathing normally again. The fever's turned!"

Jo let out a cry. "Oh Hannah, I was sure she had gone."

"She's over the worst," said Hannah, "but she's not safe yet."

Dr. Bangs came in a short time later. "She's definitely better," he announced. "But let her sleep and keep the house quiet. I think the little girl will pull through."

"If Mother would only come now," said Jo, longingly.

The snow had stopped falling and the sun rose on a beautiful morning. Jo, Meg, and

"She's over the worst."

Hannah's long vigil was over. Just then, the sound of galloping hooves could be heard outside. It was Laurie with his most precious cargo.

"It's Mother!" cried Meg and Jo, as one. "She's back! She's back!"

Chapter 15
Laurie's Mischief

There are no words to describe the joy in the house on the morning that Mrs. March returned. And, as if to make it even more joyful, Beth awoke from her long sleep. The first thing she saw was Mrs. March's face. Beth was too weak to say anything, but she smiled and nestled into her mother's loving arms.

Laurie was sent off to tell Aunt March what had happened. It was now safe to bring Amy back to the house. Aunt March would never admit it, but there was a tear in her eye when she heard that Beth had recovered.

The next day, Mrs. March gave Jo some surprising news. John Brooke, who had been looking after them in Washington, had made a confession.

"John was such a perfect boy and was so devoted to helping Father," she said. "One night he confided in me. He told me he had fallen in love with Meg."

Nestling in her mother's arms

"I knew there was mischief brewing some-where," Jo said, with a frown. "Well, he can't fall in love with her. We don't want to lose her. I would marry Meg myself just to keep her in the family."

"I know you worry about losing your sisters," said Mrs. March, "but you can't stop someone falling in love with one of them. Please, don't say a word to Meg about it. She's only sev-enteen and it'll be a long time before John can earn enough to make a home for both of them."

"Wouldn't you rather she marry a rich man?" asked Jo.

"Money is useful, Jo," said Mrs. March, "but not everything."

"I'd rather planned that Meg would marry Laurie," said Jo. "Then she could live next door and enjoy a life of luxury. Laurie's rich and good, and loves us all."

Mrs. March smiled. "Never mind Laurie. He's too young for Meg," she said. "But what do you think, Jo? Do you think Meg might care for John one day?"

"Mercy me," said Jo. "I don't know anything about love and such nonsense. In books, the girls show affection by blushing and fainting, growing thin and acting like fools. Meg doesn't do any of that."

Just then, Meg came in. She said she had just been writing a letter to John Brooke. "I wanted to thank him for looking after you in Washington," she said.

"Oh, send my love to John," said Mrs. March. "He was so kind. He was like a son to us in Washington. I have become very fond of him."

"Oh I am glad," said Meg. "He is nice but he seems so lonely. He can be a brother for us."

That night Mrs. March lay awake thinking about Meg and John. "She doesn't love John yet," she thought, "but I think she will soon learn to."

In the days that followed, Jo found it hard to keep the secret about Meg. It didn't take Laurie long to see that Jo was keeping something from him. She even admitted that she had a secret but couldn't tell him. But, she did hint that it was something about Meg and John Brooke.

The longer Jo kept the secret, the angrier Laurie became. At last, the mischievous boy took action. He wrote a bogus letter to Meg, pretending it had come from John Brooke.

"He seems so lonely."

The note professed John's love for Meg. It was cleverly written.

My dearest Meg
I have lost my heart to you. Please tell me that one day you will marry me. How happy we could be. Grandpa Laurence will help me to a good position in life. Please don't say anything about this to any of your family. But send one word of hope to me through Laurie.
Your devoted John

Meg had never been so shocked in all her life.

Chapter 16
The Plot Uncovered

When Meg recovered from the shock of receiving such a note, she wondered what to do. She decided to reply. It was a kind letter, thanking John Brooke for his affection, but saying she was far young to have thoughts of love and marriage. Rather than send the letter via Laurie, as requested in the note, she sent it directly to John.

She soon received a reply from John saying that he was very puzzled. He had never sent such a note to her. Meg knew immediately that someone was playing a trick. She dashed into the drawing room and found Jo sitting with Mrs. March.

"How could you do it, Jo?" she asked angrily.

"I've done nothing," replied Jo.

Meg took the original letter from her pocket and the reply from John, and threw them into Jo's lap.

Jo read both letters and then stood up. "Oh, the little villain!" she cried. "He's taken his revenge for my keeping a secret from him."

"What secret? Who's a villain?" asked Meg.

"Oh, nothing," said Jo, determined to keep her vow not to mention what Mrs. March had told her about John liking Meg.

Mrs. March read the letters. "Are you sure you're not involved, Jo?" she asked. "You've played plenty of pranks like this before."

"On my word, Mother," she protested.

"Oh Mother, I shall die of embarrassment," said Meg.

"There is no need," said Jo. "John will understand. He certainly didn't send the original note. But I know who did!"

With that, she dashed out of the room, crying: "I'll send the true culprit to you in a minute."

A few moments later Laurie appeared, hanging his head in shame. "I'm sorry," he said. "I wrote the letter. I did it to spite Jo because she wouldn't tell me her secret."

"Did John have anything to do with it?" asked Mrs. March.

"No," replied Laurie quietly. "It was all me."

"Thank goodness for that," sighed Meg.

Jo read both letters.

"I have behaved abominably," said Laurie. "I don't deserve to be spoken to for a month. But you will, won't you?"

Meg and Mrs. March did eventually forgive Laurie. And all of them agreed that the matter of the letter and Laurie's part in it were to be their secret. No one else was to hear about it. But Laurie's grandfather guessed that the boy had been in trouble. Laurie wouldn't admit anything and locked himself in his room, refusing to come down.

"I have behaved abominably."

An angry Grandpa Laurence then confronted Jo. All she would say was that Laurie had done something wrong, but had apologized and the matter was closed.

"Don't punish him for not telling you," she begged. "He promised along with the rest of us to keep a secret. It would hurt someone if the secret were known."

The old man calmed down a little. "If he's keeping a secret through honor rather than just being obstinate," he said, "then I'll forgive him. But he is obstinate."

"So am I," said Jo. "But all the king's horses and all the king's men couldn't drag this secret out of us."

Grandpa Laurence smiled. "I love the boy, you know. But he does try my patience."

"I'm sure Mother would say the same thing of me," replied Jo.

"Go and bring him down," said Grandpa Laurence. "Tell him all is forgiven."

Chapter 17
A Special Christmas Present

Like sunshine after a storm, peace returned to the March household as Christmas approached again. Christmas Day was ushered in with fine winter weather. Hannah looked up into the blue sky and promised it was going to be an especially "plummy" day.

There was a letter waiting from Father beneath the Christmas tree. Mrs. March read it out at breakfast. Father was getting much, much better.

Grandpa Laurence, Laurie, and John Brooke had been invited to join the family for dinner. Everyone had just sat down when Laurie appeared at the door.

"Happy Christmas everyone," he announced. "I have a special present for the March family."

Laurie stepped aside and took a bow. A man appeared in the doorway. It was Mr. March. He tried to say something, but chairs went flying as he was almost run down by a stampede of daughters and an adoring wife.

"Father!" they all cried out. Mr. March became invisible in the embrace of five pairs of loving arms. Soon everyone was kissing everyone. John Brooke even kissed Meg!

Never was there such a Christmas dinner as they had that day. The fat turkey was a sight for sore eyes! So were the plum pudding and the jellies.

That evening Meg, Jo, Beth, Amy, and Mr. and Mrs. March sat together around the roaring fire.

Mr. March looked at his girls one by one. He turned to Meg first. "I remember you when your hands were white and smooth," he began. "Now they are marked with a blemish here and there. They show how hard you have worked to help Mother. I know how much she appreciates what you do."

Next came Jo. "Where's the tomboy I left more than a year ago?" he asked. "I see a young lady now. She laces her boots and talks properly. I kind of miss my wild little daughter. She must have been the kind person who sent me twenty-five dollars when I was ill."

Mr. March looked at Beth. "You've had a

"Father!"

105

tough year, my sweet," he said, "and we can thank God that you are still with us. And you don't seem half as shy as you used to be."

Amy was next. "How good you are at helping Mother," he said. "You have learned to think of other people more than yourself. You are to be congratulated on that, *Your Ladyship*."

Amy laughed at that last remark.

Late that evening, a coach pulled up outside the house. It was Aunt March.

She hadn't come just to welcome home her nephew, Mr. March. No, she had been hearing rumors that John Brooke wanted to marry Meg.

"You can't marry him," the old lady said to Meg, as she sipped at a cup of tea. "The man has no money, no proper job. He knows you have rich relations like me. That's probably the reason for the attraction. I'll tell you now, if you marry that man, you'll not get a penny in my will."

Aunt March never realized it, but because she was so bossy, most people did exactly the opposite to what she wanted. And so it was when she ordered Meg not to marry John Brooke.

Up until that moment, Meg had not really thought about John as a possible husband. But

Ordering Meg not to marry John

Aunt March's words had made her think that perhaps she could marry him.

"I shall marry who I please," she replied. "And you can leave your money to whoever you like."

"Don't get hoity-toity with me," snapped Aunt March. "Listen to my advice or regret it for the rest of your life."

"Father and Mother like John," said Meg.

"Your pa and ma are no wiser than you are," replied the old lady. "Look how poor they are."

"I'd rather they were poor and lived in a small house," said Meg. "That's better than having lots of money and living in a great lonely house like yours."

Meg could hardly believe what she was saying. But she was glad she was defending her right to like John Brooke.

"Well, I wash my hands of you," said Aunt March. "You are a willful child. Don't expect anything from me when you marry."

With that, the old lady walked out of the room and slammed the door shut behind her.

The next day Meg went and told John what had happened. It was the best news John had heard, for he truly did love Meg a great deal.

"So you do care for me a little," he said.

"I didn't know how much," smiled Meg, "until Aunt March ordered me not to."

John kissed Meg gently on the cheek. It was a kiss witnessed by Jo and she ran to tell everyone what she had seen.

"John Brooke is acting dreadfully," she cried, "and Meg seems to like it."

Chapter 18
The Wedding

Our story of the March family must move on. It is now three years later. The war is over. Mr. March is now a minister of the local parish. Mrs. March is as cheery as ever, though her hair is a little grayer.

John Brooke did go and fight in the war. He showed great bravery on the battlefield and was injured. The young man was sent home to recover with the help of his beloved Meg. After that, he worked very hard to build a small house for them to live in when they were married.

The house John built was quickly named the *Dovecote* by Laurie. It was perfect, he said, for two people who never stopped billing and cooing like two love-sick doves. It was tiny, with a lawn the size of a small handkerchief behind it.

And what of Jo? The topsy-turvy young woman was now spinning tales like a spider

The Wedding

The Dovecote

and earning a regular dollar or two from the *Spread Eagle* magazine each month.

Jo, whose once sharp tongue had softened a touch, never went back to Aunt March's. The old lady took a shine to Amy instead.

Amy's nose never did get a point on it. She was painting more than ever now. Amy was also pretending that she hadn't noticed being chased by a young man called Parker. "Heavens above!" she said. "We can't have two weddings in the family this year."

Beth, poor thing, never really recovered fully from the fever. Yet she was everyone's friend and worked as hard as ever in the March home.

Laurie was sure that after Meg, Jo would be the next March girl to marry. The Laurence boy was now at university. Taller, richer, and better looking than most other students, he soon made lots of great friends. He often brought them home to meet the March girls.

Amy loved Laurie's friends because they were wealthy and well brought up. Of course, they liked *Her Ladyship*, but Beth was too shy to do more than peep at these boys. And Meg was too busy with marriage plans to notice them. But Jo was in her element and loved imitating their smart voices.

The Wedding

Aunt March was as irritable as ever. She was such an obstinate woman. She could never go back on her promise that she wouldn't give Meg a cent if she married John Brooke. But, anonymously, she did send the couple some fine linen for their house.

The wedding was held in June. A beautiful day dawned. The morning was spent decorating the dining room, which was to be used for both the wedding and the feast afterwards.

Meg had decided against a *fashionable* wedding. Instead, she made her own dress; a

A simple but beautiful gown

simple but beautiful gown that made her look like a charming rose. She wasn't going to mind how many people hugged her and crumpled her dress. She was just so happy.

Aunt March was scandalized when she saw the simple gown. "Upon my word," she cried, taking her seat of honor in the dining room. "Couldn't you have found something more expensive?"

"I'm not on show," said Meg. "No one has come to stare and criticize my dress. I'm going to have my little wedding just as I like it."

Deep down, Aunt March saw something of herself in Meg. Was that a tear in the old lady's eye? If it was, Aunt March quickly wiped it away as Laurie came by. "Don't let that young giant come near me," she said. "He worries me worse than mosquitoes."

There was no bridal procession. Instead, the couple and Mr. March, who was to take the service, simply gathered around an arch of fresh flowers that had been built at one end of the room. The bridegroom's hands shook. The minister's fatherly voice kept breaking into a nervous croak. And Meg quietly said: "I will."

Then she turned to the guests and cried out: "The first kiss is for Mother!"

The Wedding

"The first kiss is for Mother!"

Mrs. March did get the first kiss from the newlywed Mrs. Meg Brooke. Then for the next fifteen minutes, Meg kissed just about everyone in the room. She finally got round to kissing her husband, too.

Aunt March did get a kiss, but she took the chance to give the couple a warning. "Meg, I wish you well," she said, "but I still think you'll regret it. And you, my man, you've got a treasure. See that you deserve it!"

Laurie got some advice that day too. "If you ever want to get married," said John Brooke, "then my advice is to pick one of the March girls. You can't go wrong."

That evening, after all the guests had gone, the March family escorted Meg and John to their new house.

"Don't think that I'm separated from you now, Mother," said Meg. "I love you none the less for loving John so much. I shall come every day to see you. And I shall expect to keep my old place in all your hearts."

Meg had one last thing to say before she and John went into the house. "Thank you all for my lovely, happy wedding day."

Chapter 19

Amy Learns a Lesson

After the wedding, *Her Ladyship*, otherwise known as Miss Amy March, poured all her spare time into painting. She met some very wealthy, well connected young ladies at her regular art classes.

"Mother," she said one day, "I would like to invite my art class ladies to lunch here. Then we could sketch the river and the broken bridge. We could make the day a sort of artistic fête. They have been very kind to me. And it hasn't made a dot of difference that they are rich and I'm not."

"Well, my poor little girl," said Mrs. March, "what would you like for your lunch? Something simple? Cakes and sandwiches?"

"Good gracious no!" snorted Amy. "It will have to be something special, like chicken, ham, lobster, and salmon, with summer salads and potatoes and fresh fruit and cream afterwards. I can pay for it. I've sold several sketches recently."

"And how many ladies will there be?" she asked.

"About twelve," replied Amy.

"Bless you my child," said Mrs. March. "We'll have to hire a huge cart to bring them all to us."

"A cart!" cried Amy. "They can't travel in anything as dreadful as a cart. I shall hire a smart carriage for them. If I can't make this a day to die for, then I won't have it at all. My lady friends do not travel by horse and cart."

"I don't know why you should want to spend so much on these wealthy ladies," said Mrs. March. "I'm sure they don't really care that much for you."

"They do!" cried Amy. "I'm not like you Mother. You don't care for polite society or cultivate fashionable manners. I do. You can go through life with your hands on hips, elbows out, and your nose in the air when you see those sorts of people. That's not my style!"

Amy's description of independence was too much. Mother and daughter burst into laughter. But the day was agreed. Twelve young ladies wrote to say they would love to come and Amy spent a fortune on food. Jo, Beth,

"It will have to be something special."

Hannah, and Mrs. March all helped to prepare it. The table was set for thirteen.

The day dawned and the expensively hired coach clattered over the hill. Mrs. March was horrified, but not totally surprised, to see there was just one lady inside. Eleven well-to-do ladies had decided they had better things to do.

The helpers were immediately summoned to clear away three quarters of the food and reset the table for two, rather than thirteen. Mrs. March felt so sorry for Amy, although her daughter had brought the disaster on herself. She had guessed that the invited ladies would only have come if they had nothing better to do.

Amy stuck her nose in the air and ignored the half-smiles on her family's lips. She treated her one guest, a Miss Elliott, politely. They had lunch before touring the countryside in a buggy and talking about art.

That evening, Amy still tried to pretend how well the day had gone. "I am satisfied, despite only Miss Elliot turning up," she said. "I did all that I set out to do, and I found Miss Elliott an enjoyable companion."

Over the next few days the family had to eat up all the food left over from poor Amy's special lunch.

She treated her one guest politely.

It was some time before Amy finally admitted what a disaster the day had been and begged the whole family not to remind her of it for at least another year. Eventually all the girls, including Amy, had a good laugh about it. *Her Ladyship* had learned a good lesson.

Chapter 20
Exciting Times

Jo's literary ambitions were now reaching new heights. One of her stories won a big prize, and a hundred dollars.

"What will you do with such a fortune?" asked Amy, a little enviously.

"I shall send Beth and Mother to the seaside for a week," she said. "They both need a rest. They shall stay in the best hotel. And Beth, you must come home plump and rosy-cheeked again."

Mrs. March protested, saying that Jo should spend the money on herself. But Jo would have none of it. So Mother and Beth did go on holiday together, and had a wonderful time. Afterwards, Mrs. March said she felt ten years younger.

Jo was writing at a great pace now. She received several large checks for her romances. Amy encouraged her on. "The more you write, the more money you will make," she said.

Father interrupted. "You must write good books—books that you believe in," he said. "The money should be an afterthought."

All thoughts about books vanished when, soon after, there was another joyous moment in the history of the March family. Meg was going to have a baby and everyone was looking forward to the happy event. There was great excitement when twins arrived, a girl and a boy. Meg and John named them Daisy and Danny.

The next big surprise was for Amy. Aunt March invited her to join her on a tour of Europe.

"Will we go to Rome?" asked Amy.

"Of course," said Aunt March.

"Good!" said Amy. "If I can't find fame in Rome with my paintings, then I shall come home and give up art forever. But I think I will find fame there. Perhaps in a year or two, I'll send for you, Jo, and we can live in a big Italian villa. I'll paint and you can write."

Amy retained her confidence until she found herself boarding the ship for Europe with Aunt March. She suddenly realized that soon a whole ocean would separate her from her family. Tears poured down Amy's cheeks as the ship hooted and she waved them farewell.

Jo, still a little miffed about not being asked

Jo was writing at a great pace now.

to go to Europe, retired to her writing room—a loft high up in the house that she called her "garret". Still, she couldn't help but read the postcards that kept arriving from Amy.

Walked down Piccadilly in London today, took a ride in a Hansom cab, and saw Buckingham Palace. Rode across Hyde Park with a duchess this morning.

Next it was France. *Visited the Louvre art gallery today. I expect they'll hang one of my paintings here one day.*

And on to Germany. *Sailed down the River Rhine and danced in Berlin. Aunt March grumpy as ever.*

Then Austria. *Went skiing today. Aunt choked on her apple strudel.*

But if Amy was having a wonderful time, the family at home was concerned about Beth.

Mrs. March came to Jo one day and asked whether she knew if anything was bothering Beth. "She sits alone all the while," she sighed. "That's not like Beth. It worries me."

Jo promised to try and find out. "I think she is just growing up," she said. "She's beginning to dream dreams. She's eighteen now; a woman, not a child any more."

Amy waved them farewell.

That afternoon, Jo was sitting with Beth when Laurie came in. Jo saw Beth's eyes follow him closely. "Mercy on me!" thought Jo. "She's lovesick. That's what the matter with her. Beth's in love with Laurie. Oh dear, we are all growing up with a vengeance."

Jo's idea that Beth was in love with Laurie brought her another heartache. That was because she suspected that Laurie was really in love with her. She decided to try and get Beth to talk about it. "Beth, have you fallen in love with Laurie?" she asked.

"Have you fallen in love with Laurie?"

"What! Me in love with Laurie?" cried Beth. "No, I love him dearly, but he will always be a favorite brother to me. That's all."

"How odd," said Jo. "You've been so quiet just recently. Here was I thinking that you were miserable because you were in love with Laurie and he didn't love you."

"Dear Jo, I do have some problems which one day I will tell you about," said Beth. "But Laurie is not one of them. Anyway, doesn't he love you?"

"I suspect he might," Jo said quietly. "But, like you, I love him as a brother and nothing else. He doesn't make my heart flutter."

"I'm glad to hear it," said Beth. "You're both rebels, too fond of freedom. You are too much alike to marry."

Jo was glad to hear Beth's views. But even Jo had no idea how strong Laurie's love for her had grown.

Chapter 21
Tantrums

One morning, Laurie finally revealed the strength of his feelings for Jo.

"It's no use hiding things any more," he said, cornering her.

'What do you mean?" asked Jo.

"The truth is, Jo," he said, "I've loved you ever since I've known you. Tell me you love me too. I'm sure you do."

Jo was astonished. She didn't know what to say for a moment. "Laurie," she said at last, "there is no one on earth I like better than you. You know how much I adore you. We have grown up together. You're the favorite brother I never had."

"But I love you . . ." stuttered Laurie.

"But I don't love you in that way," replied Jo. "However much I could try, it's impossible for someone to make themselves love someone if they don't."

"I don't believe you!" said Laurie.

"But I love you …"

"You've got to be sensible and reasonable about this," begged Jo.

"I won't be sensible and reasonable," sulked Laurie. "You haven't got a heart, Jo!"

"Yes I have!" replied Jo sharply.

"Please," begged Laurie. "Everyone expects us to marry one day. Grandpa has set his heart on it. So have your mother and sisters, I'm sure. So just say 'Yes' and we can be happy."

Jo was not a cruel person. She knew that Laurie would simply suffer a longer heartache if he didn't accept what she was saying. "You'll get over me in a while," she said. "You'll meet some beautiful girl who will love you."

"Never!" said Laurie. "I will never get over you."

With that, Laurie turned from her and walked to the door.

"Where are you going?" asked Jo.

"To the devil!" he shouted, storming out of the house.

Soon after that incident, Jo decided to pursue a lifelong ambition: to go and spend some time living in New York. "It'll give Laurie a chance to get me out of his mind," she thought.

Everyone except Laurie thought it was a wonderful idea. Jo was to stay with Mrs. Kirke, an old friend of Mrs. March. She would be a nursery teacher to the woman's two children.

Jo found it very difficult to say goodbye to her family, but the farewell with Laurie was even worse. His eyes made one last appeal for her to stay. But seeing Jo was still determined to leave, he turned away from her in a huff.

"Laurie!" cried Jo.

"It's all right," he said, "don't mind me."

But it wasn't all right. Jo did mind. She felt as if she had stabbed her best friend. And when he walked away without looking back, she knew their friendship would never be the same again.

***

Jo enjoyed life in New York with Mrs. Kirke and her children. Now, the March family had two streams of letters arriving at the house each week. Amy never stopped writing home and Jo was just the same.

Early on, Jo mentioned a professor; a lecturer in philosophy who was also lodging at the Kirke's. Jo described him as good-looking with a bushy beard, and wrote that he was much older than her. She said that he loved children and was the owner of the kindest pair of eyes she had ever seen.

Hardly a letter arrived without a mention of the Professor Bower. First came the news that he wasn't married. The next letter noted that Jo was now taking philosophy lessons with him. She also wrote that although he was poor, he always seemed to be giving something away to some needy person. He was, she said, the kindest man she had ever met.

Mrs. March was beginning to suspect that there was more to the relationship between Jo and Professor Bower than her darling daughter was revealing.

During those first months in New York, Jo also met Mr. Dashwood, editor of the *Weekly Volcano*. This was a magazine of low repute. Nevertheless, he managed to persuade Jo to write some stories for him.

Jo took to studying the newspapers and based her tales on stories she read inside them. She was astonished to discover she could write sensational stories about murder and mayhem on the streets of New York. Mr. Dashwood took every story she wrote, but only paid her a few cents for each one.

Jo made sure that the professor never saw her stories. She was too ashamed of those *Weekly Volcano* tales. Whenever they met, she

Jo enjoyed life in New York.

imagined that he could read the words *Weekly Volcano* emblazoned across her forehead!

Finally, the time came for Jo to return home. Professor Bower took her to the railway station.

"You know," he said suddenly, "I've enjoyed reading your stories. Most of my pupils read the *Weekly Volcano*."

Jo went scarlet with embarrassment; how had he found out? But she still found herself saying: "If you are ever down our way, do drop in. The family would love to meet you."

Chapter 22
Beth's Secret

When Jo came home that spring, she was glad to see that Laurie had gone off with his grandpa to Europe for a while. Word was sent ahead to Amy. The plan was for Amy and Laurie to meet in Nice, France, on the Mediterranean coast.

Jo was hugely discouraged to see that Beth's spirits seemed worse than ever. She was paler and a little thinner too. No one at home seemed to have noticed it. Perhaps it was because the changes had happened so slowly for those who saw her every day.

Jo was now determined to find out what was wrong. She managed to persuade Beth to spend two weeks on the coast with her. They were to stay with a friend of Mrs. March.

Jo and Beth spent every minute together on that holiday. They hardly dared to be parted. It was as if, by instinct, they both knew a long separation was not far away.

Beth finally told Jo everything one afternoon, as she lay beside her sister on the beach. They were looking out to sea with the breeze floating through their hair and the waves making music at their feet.

Jo quickly understood. Beth said that during the winter she had seen the doctor again. Her future, he'd said, was bleak.

"I'm glad I've told you," Beth sighed. "I tried to tell you before, but I couldn't."

Jo looked at Beth, hoping to see signs that what she was saying couldn't be true. Yet, she reminded herself of how thin Beth had become. Her hands weren't even strong enough now to hold the seashells they had collected that day.

Jo knew then that Beth was slowly drifting away from her. She put her arms around her sister and hugged her tightly. Beth was Jo's dearest treasure.

"I've known it for some time now," said Beth. "I'm used to the idea."

"Oh, why didn't you tell me earlier?" cried Jo. "How could you face this all alone?"

"It would have been unfair to frighten Mother," said Beth. "She had so many other things to worry about."

Beth finally told Jo everything.

Then Beth began to cry. "My life is like the tide, Jo," she said. "It has turned. It is going out slowly and can't be stopped."

"I'll stop it," said Jo. "I'll do anything in the world to stop it going out."

"It's too late," poor Beth continued. "But I'm sure I won't suffer for too long. The tide will go out easily for me, I think. Still, there is something you can do. The rest of the family doesn't know yet. Please tell them what I have told you. I can't bear to make them so unhappy, but I don't want to keep any secrets from my family."

"I'll promise I'll do that for you," replied Jo solemnly.

"I don't think I was ever intended to live long," said Beth. "I'm not like the rest of you. I never made any plans for what I might do when I grew up. I never thought about being married as you all did. I never wanted to go away like you and Amy have done. But the hard part now is that soon I will have to go away from you. I think I'll even feel homesick for you all when I'm in heaven."

Jo could not speak for a while. Her head was so full of sad thoughts. For a moment, there was no sound except the sigh of the wind and the lapping of the tide. Suddenly, a white-winged gull flew by, with a flash of sunshine on its silvery breast. Beth watched it until it vanished. Her eyes were full of sadness.

"That gull was you, Jo," said Beth, "strong and wild, fond of a storm, happy to be alone and flying out to sea. Meg is a sweet turtle-dove and Amy is the lark that sings in the morning."

"And which bird are you?" asked Jo.

Beth pointed to a tiny little sand-bird that was "peeping" happily close by and enjoying the sun and the sea. "Mother used to say they reminded her of me," she said, "because they were such busy little creatures and always chirping away."

Jo laughed as the little bird came quite close to Beth. It perched on a stone and started cleaning its feathers. But all the time it was looking at Beth with a friendly eye.

Beth smiled too. She felt comforted because the tiny thing seemed to be offering its friendship. It reminded her that although she did not have much time left, there was still a pleasant world to enjoy to the end.

At the end of the two weeks, Jo and Beth returned home. Beth was very tired and went straight to bed. Jo gathered all her strength

"That gull was you, Jo."

together to tell the family the tragic news. But she was spared the difficult task.

As she entered the drawing room, Mrs. March stretched out her arms to Jo as if asking for help. Without a word, Jo went to comfort her. She had already guessed the truth.

Chapter 23
Laurie and Amy

The news about Beth was kept from Amy. It was felt that there was no point in her coming home yet. And nobody wanted to spoil her time in Europe.

It was Christmas Day when Laurie met Amy on Nice's famous promenade, in France.

"Oh I thought you'd never arrive!" she cried.

Amy was so excited to see Laurie. She was enjoying her European tour but was very happy to see a kindly face from home. Yet, she quickly noticed a big change in Laurie. She had heard by letter about his proclamations of love for Jo, and how she had turned him away.

Laurie now seemed sulky, with little interest in anything. In the days that followed he seemed to laze around all the time, feeling sorry for himself.

Amy, like the rest of the March family, had always been very fond of Laurie. She was sad

Laurie and Amy

Amy was so excited to see Laurie.

to see the change in him. But while they were together in France, they began to see each other in a different light.

Laurie found himself enjoying Amy's company, even if he was still sulking and taking her affection for granted. They never quarreled. Amy was too well bred for that and Laurie was too lazy to get into an argument. But day by day, Amy began to lose patience with Laurie's attitude.

"When are you going back?" she asked one morning.

"I think I'll hang around," he yawned. "I'd rather stay and plague you. By the way, have you begun your great work of art yet?"

"I never will," said Amy. "My time in Rome and seeing all the great works there convinced me that my art will be just too insignificant. I want to be great or nothing. So I'm afraid my life as an artist is at an end."

"So what will you do now?" asked Laurie.

"I shall probably marry some wealthy man and be a wifely ornament on his arm," she replied. "But at least I will still be doing more than your lazing and moping around, thinking of Jo."

"That's rich coming from you," snorted

Laurie. "All you want to be in life is a society queen. That's not doing much!"

"What would Jo think if she saw you now?" continued Amy, starting to lose her temper. "She'd have a new name for you, *Lazy Laurie.* You've been given everything: good looks, money, and oodles of charm. Yet you're just throwing everything away!"

Amy had now lost her temper completely. "And just look at your hands," she cried. "They are as pale and soft as a girl's. It looks as if you've never done anything with them other than put on fine woolen gloves. Aren't you ashamed of hands like that? You're a real dandy!"

Laurie was silenced. He knew Amy was right. "Do you think Jo would despise me if she saw me now?"

"Yes! She hates lazy people," said Amy, calming down a little.

"She's the one that hurt me," said Laurie. "It wasn't the other way around."

"Love Jo all you want," said Amy, "but don't let it spoil your whole life. If you really want her, go and win her. Fight for her."

It didn't take Laurie and Amy long to forget their argument. Amy's lecture had done the

"You're a real dandy!"

trick. For the rest of his time in Nice, Laurie took Amy everywhere. They had such a nice time together.

And the most surprising thing of all was that when Laurie left Nice to travel around other parts of Europe, Amy missed him so very much.

Chapter 24
The Saddest Day

The March family was deeply upset about Beth's illness. They set apart the best room in the house for her, and in it they put everything she most loved—flowers, Amy's loveliest sketches, her little piano, and her beloved three cats. Every day, Meg brought the twins to see her. Hannah never wearied of cooking her favorite foods.

Even as she was preparing to leave life, Beth still tried to make it happier for those who would stay behind. She loved watching children outside her window as they passed by on their way to school. She started knitting woolen mittens for the poorest schoolchildren.

Jo stayed with her for just about every minute of each day. As Beth slept, she would write poems.

One day, it was Jo's turn to fall asleep. Her latest poem was lying on the floor. Beth picked it up and read it. It was a long poem in praise

She loved watching children.

of Beth's courage, kindness, serenity, and patience. But there were four lines that she liked best:

> *Oh, my sister, passing from me,*
> *Out of human care and strife,*
> *Leave me, as a gift, those virtues*
> *Which have beautified your life.*

Those words brought huge comfort to Beth. She had always thought she had done so little in life. She had assumed her life had been a useless one.

"Thank you for that poem," she said when Jo awoke. "I don't think that I've wasted my life any more. I'm not as good as you say I am in the poem, but I have tried to do right. It is a great comfort to know that someone loves me and feels I have helped them."

"I love you more than anyone in the world," said Jo. "Even death will never part us."

"It cannot," said Beth. "Our love can only grow. And you must take my place, Jo. Be everything to Mother and Father when I'm gone. And remember, love is the only thing we can carry with us when we go."

So the spring days came and went and the

sky grew bluer and the earth greener. Summer flowers arrived early to say goodbye to Beth. As Beth had hoped, her "tide" went out peacefully and Jo held her hand to the last.

These were dark days for all the March family. Poor Jo was heartbroken over Beth's death. But, as ever, it was Mother who came to her rescue in the end.

"Jo, why don't you start writing again," she said. "That always used to make you happy. Forget the rest of the world. Just write a story for our family; something we'll all enjoy."

And that's what Jo did. She retired to her lonely garret and wrote one of those stories that went straight to everyone's heart. Meg and Jo and their parents laughed and cried their way through the story. Only Jo knew that Beth had been sitting on her shoulder, helping her to write it.

Mr. March sent the story to a magazine. To Jo's surprise, the story was published and paid for. Better still, the magazine wanted more of her stories.

So, taught by love and sorrow, Jo became a full-time writer. She was soon writing for several different magazines.

***

Jo held her hand to the last.

As time passed, Jo's heart started to mend.
And Laurie's too. When Laurie and Amy
returned to America they spent a lot of time
together. They had heard the sad news of Beth
while in Europe and rushed home as soon as
they could.

Amy had dreaded going home, much as
she longed to see her family. She couldn't
bear to think of returning to a house empty of
Beth. Laurie had been a great support and as
time passed their friendship grew stronger and

The story went straight to everyone's heart.

155

stronger. Laurie still loved Jo, but in Amy he found a good friend.

One day, Laurie was rowing Amy across a lake when he started to tire.

"Let me row a little way," said Amy.

"I'm not so very tired," he replied, "but you can take one oar if you like."

So Amy moved herself to Laurie's side and took one of the oars. Laurie counted them off. "One, two, three . . . row!"

Neither spoke for a few minutes as they rowed themselves across the lake. Then Amy broke the silence. "How well we pull together, don't we?" she said.

"So well," answered Laurie, "that it would be nice if we could always row in the same boat. What do you say, Amy?"

The faintest of blushes spread across Amy's face.

Chapter 25
A Knock at the Door

It wasn't long before *Her Ladyship* and *His Lordship*, as Amy called Laurie, announced they wanted to marry. Amy said to Mother: "I love him so much because he lets me read his heart."

What she meant was that Laurie had opened his heart to her love.

Jo was happy for them both; best of all because she now had her good friend back. She and Laurie could be like loving brother and sister again. Yet, as the months passed, she wondered if she was now doomed to spend a lonely life writing in her garret.

Jo had even forgotten—well, almost—an invitation she had once given to someone during her days in New York. "If you are ever down our way, do drop in. The family would love to meet you," she had said.

So Jo was very surprised indeed when that someone knocked on her door and she found

Professor Bower on the doorstep. At first she was struck dumb with shyness. But by the time she had introduced him to all the family, she was talking excitedly to him. She suddenly realized how much she had missed this lonely man.

It didn't take the family long to find out why Jo liked the professor so much. He was one of those people who knocks on a stranger's door and immediately finds himself at home.

Meg's twins fell in love with him. All the women in the house nodded their instant approval, while Grandpa Laurence became a soul mate. The professor even joined in a singing duet with Amy. Jo had no more idea about music than a grasshopper, but she clapped long and hard when they finished.

That evening, Jo wondered what business had brought Professor Bower to the area. How foolish could the girl be? His business concerned Miss Josephine March, of course!

In truth, the professor's visit wasn't only to see Jo. He had just been appointed to teach in a nearby college. But it was Laurie who saw his real purpose first. "That man," he announced to Amy, "intends to marry our Jo."

"Yes," agreed Amy. "And I really hope he does. Will that hurt you?"

Professor Bower was on the doorstep.

"Not at all," replied Laurie. "I have my darling Amy now. But, for Jo's sake, it would be nice if the professor was a little bit richer and younger."

"Women should never marry for money," replied Amy. Then she remembered two things. First, she had once boasted she would marry a rich man, and second, she *was* actually going to marry a rich man.

"Oops," she laughed. "But of course, I would still marry you if you were penniless!"

"And I should think so, *Your Ladyship*!" said His Lordship.

Within a couple of weeks, everyone knew perfectly well what was going on between Jo and Professor Bower.

One morning, Jo decided to go into town to do some shopping. It was threatening to rain, but she was in such a dizzy mood that she forgot to take an umbrella. No sooner had she reached the center of town than the heavens opened. The rain poured down. Head down, Jo ran for cover, scurrying across the road that was quickly turning to mud.

How she missed being run over by a passing truck, she never knew. But the next thing, she had collided with a gentleman, sending him head-first into the mud.

The man recovered and got to his feet. "Well, Miss March," said Professor Bower, wiping the mud from his smiling face. "How nice to see you!"

Jo felt very foolish. What must the professor have thought of her? He didn't mind, of course. He found it all very funny. And, to make things better, he put his arm in hers and walked her to the nearest shelter from the rain. She felt as if the sun had suddenly come out.

Their friendship blossomed that summer. She continued with her writing. He came over to the house whenever he could. Jo learned much from Professor Bower's huge knowledge and experience of the world. Why, he could speak several languages fluently and discuss Shakespeare at the drop of a hat!

He always used to say to Jo: "I have no fortune, except a bit of learning."

And Jo was always glad to sit at his knee borrowing some of his knowledge.

Then, on another wet day, something else happened. The professor was holding an umbrella over Jo's head in the middle of town. A lot of people were milling around. Jo, precocious as ever, felt a powerful need to kiss him.

"How nice to see you!"

The crowd was not going to put her off. She turned and planted her lips on his.

So, finally, Jo had let love in. She had also shut the door behind it, just to make sure it didn't escape.

Chapter 26
Plumfield

It wasn't long before Amy and Laurie were married, much to the family's delight. Soon after, Jo and her professor were also married in a wonderful, happy ceremony. Then, suddenly, there was another death in the family. This one truly set Jo on the path to her dream.

Jo's secret wish had been to open a school for poor young boys. She wanted a good home-like school, where youngsters could be taken care of and taught at the same time. She already had her head teacher — Professor Bower.

Then Aunt March died, and in her will she left Jo her rambling old house, which was called Plumfield. It was only in death that Aunt March could show Jo how much she had truly loved her.

So now Jo had her school too.

Laurie reckoned it would cost a fortune to run the house as a school. "Where will you get the money if you are only having poor boys that can't pay?" he asked.

"Oh, there'll be rich children as well," she said. "Rich children often need as much care and love at school as the poor. Just look at you, Laurie! Haven't I brought up one rich boy to be the pride and joy of his family?"

"You tried to," replied Laurie, with a smile.

"Come on, admit it," insisted Jo. "I succeeded beyond my dreams with you. I am proud of you and each year you get better.

She left Jo her rambling old house.

You'll see. When I have my boys at school, I'll point you out and tell them to follow your example. You'll be their model."

Laurie blushed as red as a beetroot.

An astonishing year followed. Jo soon had a family of ten boys to look after while the professor taught them. Some were poor and some were rich. There was a waiting list, but Jo always squeezed one more into her very special academy if she could.

Every room in Aunt March's old house was soon full, and every plot in the garden had an owner. Pets were allowed, so a regular menagerie of animals now filled the sheds.

Jo even managed to squeeze two boys of her own into the crowded house. Jo and the professor became the proud parents of Rob and Teddy.

Plumfield was never a fashionable school and Jo and Professor Bower never made a fortune out of it. It was, as Jo intended, a happy home and school in one.

Would poor Aunt March have lamented her old house being overrun with Toms, Dicks, and Harrys? There was some poetic justice about it all because the lady had been the terror of all the boys for miles around. Now they freely

An astonishing year followed.

feasted on her plums, kicked up her gravel path, and played football on her meadow.

Then, perhaps, in her own secret way, Aunt March might actually have liked to see young people enjoying her property. Of course, she would never have admitted it.

Chapter 27
Harvest Home!

Plumfield School was a great success. And one of the nicest things about it was that Jo made sure that Professor Bower gave the boys plenty of holidays.

The annual apple-picking season in autumn was always the most popular holiday. On the occasion of Jo's fifth wedding anniversary, everyone gathered for this enjoyable fruit festival. The old orchard was wearing its autumn holiday dress, crickets chirped noisily, and squirrels were busy with their own harvest.

Mother and Father March led the family into the orchard. Next were Meg, her husband John and their twins, Daisy and Danny. Close behind were Jo and the professor, and their boys, Rob and Teddy. Amy and Laurie were there with their two babies. Then there was Hannah and Grandpa Laurence.

Finally, there were all the boys from Plumfield School, chattering excitedly amongst themselves.

It was a perfect October day. Everybody laughed and sang, played, climbed up trees, and tumbled down again. Between the playing, they picked all the apples. Soon there were piles of apples everywhere. Mrs. March and Meg sat sorting them out.

Mr. March, Grandpa Laurence, and the professor discussed philosophy, while Laurie devoted most of the day to the youngsters. He carried his youngest child around in an apple basket.

Jo's Teddy led a charmed life. He was a chip off the old block; Jo's block. She had been a wild tomboy as a child. Teddy was worse. But Jo never worried if a lad whisked him up a tree, or another galloped off with the child on his back. She knew Teddy would turn up safe again.

Later on, Jo and Meg laid out the harvest supper on the grass. It was a feast of pies, cookies, and apple turnovers.

As the sun began to set on that wonderful day, Professor Bower raised his glass of home-made lemonade to give the first toast.

"To Aunt March," he cried. "God bless her!"

The professor never forgot how much he, Jo and the Plumfield boys owed to the old lady.

Harvest Home!

A perfect October day

Next, there was a toast from Grandpa Laurence to mark Mrs. March's sixtieth birthday. "A long life" was his toast to the mother of the harvest feast.

There were presents for everyone. There were so many that they had to be carried to the feast in a wheelbarrow. Every one had been handmade. There was one special present that Amy had made in memory of a lost sister. It was a handkerchief for Mrs. March. On it Amy had embroidered seven words:

To dear Mother, from her little Beth

It brought tears to Mrs. March's eyes. "I believe dear Beth is with us today," she said quietly to Mr. March.

When this was going on, the boys of Plumfield School had quietly sneaked away towards a great elm tree. It was always known as the Harvest Feasting Tree.

While Mrs. March was still wiping away her tears, the professor suddenly stepped forward and began to sing. It was a beautiful tune and the words were taken from the poem that Jo had written for Beth.

172

Harvest Home!

Oh, my sister, passing from me,
Out of human care and strife,
Leave me, as a gift, those virtues
Which have beautified your life.

After the professor had sung the first verse, hidden voices high up in the elm tree echoed out above him. Everyone looked up, but the tree choir was hidden from view by the last leaves of summer.

This event was Professor Bower's special surprise and everyone was quite moved by it. But Jo, for one, was happy when all her boys were safely back on the ground.

Now it was Mother's turn to make a toast. She thanked all her daughters for their love and the grandchildren they had given her. Then she turned to Jo and the Plumfield boys. "Thanks to you Jo, these boys have a chance. This is your harvest, and it is a good one."

Jo interrupted her. "Mother," she said, pointing to her sisters, "it's not as good a harvest as yours. Just look at us all. We are all your harvest. We cannot thank you enough for the patient sowing, reaping, and nurturing you have done over the years."

Touched to the heart, Mrs. March could

Professor Bower's special surprise.

do nothing but shed more tears and sob out a thank you. "Oh my girls," she said, "however long you may live, remember this day. You have made me the happiest woman alive."

"Father once called you his Little Women. Now you are good wives. Jo has her boys. They will grow up into Little Men. No doubt, one day someone will write a story about you and all your families.

"But for me, for however long I live, you will always be my lovely girls. So one last toast: To the happiness of my own Little Women."

The End